This book of "Tails" belongs to:

____

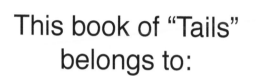

We hope you enjoy reading about our
Allagash Adventures!

Tim Caverly
Franklin Manzo, Jr.

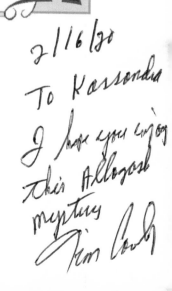

2/16/20
To Kassandra
I hope you enjoy
this Allagash
mystery
Tim Caverly

Allagash Tails Collection - Volume Two

Tales From A National Wild and Scenic River

An Allagash Haunting

The Story of Emile Camile

(Book One of Olivia's Journey)

by

Tim Caverly

Illustrated by

Franklin Manzo, Jr.

Leicester Bay
BOOKS

Newport, Maine

Library of Congress Cataloging-in-Publication Data
Caverly, Tim.
ALLAGASH TAILS: A collection of short stories from Maine's Allagash Wilderness Waterway
Vol. II:
An Allagash Haunting/ The Story of Emile Camile/
By Tim Caverly;
Illustrated by Franklin Manzo, Jr.
p. cm. - (Emile)
"Tim Caverly"

Summary: A Canoe trip with her family down Maine's Allagash Wilderness Waterway leads to a haunting adventure for 10-year-old Olivia.

Printed in the U.S.A.
First Printing, October 2009
ISBN 978-1-4507-1271-2
Leicester Bay Books, Second Edition, February 2018
ISBN-13: 978-1985598027
ISBN-10: 1985598027

The books of
TIM CAVERLY
Illustrated by **FRANKLIN MANZO, JR.**

The Allagash Tails Collection

Volume 1: **Allagash Tails – Marvin & Charlie, OR Duck Meets Beaver** (Illustrated Children's Book)
Volume 2: **An Allagash Haunting: The Story Of Emile Camile** (Book Three of Olivia's Journey)
Volume 3: **Wilderness Wildlife** (Illustrated Children's Book)
Volume 4: **The Wilderness Ranger's Journal – Rendezvous at Devil's Elbow** (Book Three of Olivia's Journey)
Volume 5: **Headin' North: A Tale of Two Diaries** (Book Three of Olivia's Journey)
Volume 6: **Solace**
Volume 7: **The Ranger and the Reporter**
Volume 8: **Andy's Surprise** (Illustrated Children's Book)

Available through
www.allagashtails.com and www.leicesterbaybooks.com

<u>Also by Tim Caverly</u>

An Allagash Haunting: The Story of Emile Camile (The play - with songs) (with Barbara Howe Hogan)

Available through
www.leicesterbaytheatricals.com

TABLE OF CONTENTS

NOTE: There are words highlighted in **bold** throughout the story. These words are vocabulary words for which you can find definitions in the Glossary at the back of the book.

ACKNOWLEDGEMENTS

At first it appeared that writing my first chapter book for classroom use would be a simple task. All I had to do was put my thoughts and experiences on paper, or so I thought. I soon learned that composing a story was much more complicated than that. There were moments when ideas refused to come. Then there was the seemingly endless editing; repairing run on sentences; ensuring subject-verb agreement, and ensuring the proper use of descriptive language. Then I had to find a way for it to be printed, which seemed financially prohibitive. It didn't take long to realize that it takes the support of talented and generous people to create a tale interesting enough to be read over and over.

The following are unselfish folks who graciously contributed their time to this story. Without their help and encouragement, this work would not have been possible:

Thank you to teachers Lindsay Luetje of Telstar Regional Middle High School in Bethel; Terry Murphy of Lubec Middle School; Andrea Edwards of Katahdin Middle School; Pauline Hanley of Medway Middle School; Lexie Hartung of Granite Street School; Therese Inman, Mary Kittrick and Beth Peavey of Millinocket Middle School, Theresa Cyr of Madawaska Middle High School; Bob Tinkham of Millinocket, Clair Moriarty of Bangor, and

Patty Smith of Belmont, N.H.
A debt of gratitude also goes out to Louise Pelletier–Maine author, and Master Maine Guide–Gil Gilpatrick, illustrator–Franklin Manzo, Jr., and Representative Herbie Clark.

DEDICATION

This book is dedicated to:
My mother-in-law, Joan King,
who's always said
"You should write a book."

And to
Susan,
The spirit in my life.

FORWARD

My messing around with ghosts goes back many years. It wasn't something I sought out – it just sort of happened. When you are not looking to find the existence of a ghost, you tend to be slow to realize that you are, or have been, in the presence of a spirit. That is what happened to my friend Dick and me when we obtained the ownership of an old trapper's log cabin situated so deep in the Maine woods that it was not road accessible. You have to canoe or walk several miles to reach it.

We learned that the old cabin was built

in the early twentieth century by a man with the first name of Harry. As time went by, we noticed things missing or mysteriously moved from where we knew we had left them. Because of the remoteness of the cabin, we could only blame each other, or…?

Most of the things that Harry moved or took were later recovered, but his biggest prank remains a mystery to this day. Dick was at the cabin with some guests. They were using binoculars to watch moose from the front of the camp. Dick put the binoculars down on the woodpile and they all left to do a little fishing. When they returned to the camp, the binoculars were gone! He searched the rest of the day and even tore down the woodpile, thinking they had somehow fallen to the bottom of the pile. The binoculars have not been recovered to this day.

I could go on and on with Harry's hijinks, but I want to move on to the Allagash and tell you about some other ghosts that I became involved with. In guiding several trips a year through the Allagash Wilderness Waterway, I became fascinated with a place on the lower river called Ghost Landing Bar. As I was researching my book *Allagash*, I learned how the otherwise unimpressive spot became a name on the map.

In the earliest days of logging along

the waterway it was pine that the loggers were after. Before crosscut saws came into use in the Maine woods; trees were cut down with axes. The men that used the axes were called choppers. Their skill with an axe was legendary and it made them the elite of the woods crew. But accidents do happen. A chopper working on a large pine didn't notice the tree twisting on its stump as it started to fall. The tree fell on the chopper and killed him. In due time, the log from the tree was moved to the water's edge where it was to be floated downriver to the mill. However, it was discovered that the pine had a hollow heart, so the log was never rolled into the water but left there to rot. For years after, it was reported that the ghost of the chopper was seen sitting on the log beseeching all who passed to roll the log into the river so his spirit could be at peace.

The exploits of the ghost of Ghost Landing Bar became the subject of several articles I wrote. It seems the ghost became bored with sitting there on the log and started traveling up and down the waterway making comments and suggestions as he went along.

And probably doing some mischief as well, just to entertain himself. One day I was having coffee in the waterway headquarters with my friends Tim and Susan Caverly. We were talking about the ghost stories and it was there that I learned about another ghost haunting the waterway. Emile Camile!

I could hardly wait to write the story of Emile and tell what this wonderful little man did to keep good cheer and high spirits in the little community of Churchill Depot in the early 1900's. Imagine my surprise when, a few weeks after the article was published, I received a letter from Mrs. Emile Camile. She thanked me for writing about her "dear Emile" and told me some things I wish I had known earlier. You will read her letter on your journey through this wonderful story.

People from all over the world are aware of the Allagash. The name seems to evoke a desire in people to know more about it. People from all over the United States as well as several other countries have contacted me to travel on and learn about our legendary waterway. Now, thanks to Tim, there is something for young people to read about our beloved Allagash. I know his stories will whet the appetite for more knowledge and a desire to protect and preserve this valuable Maine heritage.

Have a good read and enjoy!

—Gil Gilpatrick 2009

Gil Gilpatrick is a Master Maine Guide, a life member of the Maine Professional Guides Association, a founding member of the Maine Wilderness Guides Organization. He has served as a member of the Advisory Board for the Licensing of Guides since 1996. He is a member of the New England Outdoor Writers Association and is the author of seven outdoor-related books. He has been canoeing on the Allagash since 1972 and has been an outdoor columnist since1979.

INTRODUCTION

I am not sure if I really know when I first got the idea for this story. For several years I have been thinking about writing something fresh about the Allagash, a topic that hadn't already been covered.

Information about this infamous waterway is so well documented that I wasn't sure where to start. The real beginning of this story was the book released in the spring of 2009, *Allagash Tails Vol. 1.* Those stories were based on the animal antics that my family and I witnessed during the eighteen years that we lived on the Allagash Wilderness Waterway. I wrote about those observations, rather than surf TV trying to find something on, in children's story format as a treat for my daughter when she was very small.

This past winter I decided to have a couple of the stories illustrated as a Christmas gift for my daughter and her husband. The artistry of Franklin Manzo, Jr., brought the tales to life so well that we decided to print a few to see if others might like them.

In the spring of 2009 I was invited to read one of the stories aloud in Mrs. Steven's Sixth-grade ELA class at the

Millinocket Middle School. This was the first public reading. As I read the tale "Marvin the Merganser," Mrs. Stevens, in game-show-hostess fashion, presented the illustrations. All eyes were on us.

At the end of class, several pupils came to us and said they enjoyed the story so much they wondered if I would help them write a story. Perhaps that is where *An Allagash Haunting* really started. I thought that if I wrote a story about a place in Maine, then students might be encouraged to read, learn new vocabulary words and write creatively.

So I guess the real credit for this story goes out to those students who planted the seed that grew into this tale of my daughter, son-in-law, and granddaughter taking a future trip down the Allagash.

Tim Caverly
September, 2009
Millinocket, Maine

PREFACE
Ghosts, Ghouls and Déjà Vu

Do you believe in ghosts? Have you ever seen one? I have, many times. I witness ghosts and ghouls every Halloween as children and adults put on costumes to mimic some "out of this world" spirit. But do these spirits really exist? If they do, where do they live and can they visit us? Since the beginning of time these questions have been studied by people fascinated by the **paranormal** activity of shadowy images. For **generations** debate has flourished over the possibility of a parallel universe where spirits are transported from their place of darkness to our land of light. But how can that happen?

In science, we learn that energy converts from one form to another. This is also true with organisms. For example, when a tree dies, it changes into a source of nourishment so that new trees and vegetation can grow. This is the cycle of life. So in the **progression** of living beings, can human energy also convert from one form to another? Evolving towards a **sequence** of events that directs our past to collide with our present? Someplace so far away, yet so close, words already spoken are waiting to be reborn?

This perception or idea is sometimes

called **déjà vu**. As defined by Webster's dictionary déjà vu *is the feeling people have from time to time of having been in a place or experienced something before.*

Perhaps the most common example of *déjà vu* is when an individual meets someone they have never seen before, but it feels as if he or she has always known the other person. As they talk, something clicks and one of the people feels a flashback and thinks; *I've experienced this before.* This higher level of consciousness happens so quickly that the person shivers as he or she declares, "That's really strange!"

Mention this **phenomenon** to others and inevitably there is an astonished response of, "I've had the same thing happen to me." Words, places, smells, or everyday objects can cause this awareness of another presence or reality. Perhaps this experience supports the theory that a corresponding energy level, or that a mirror image exists where things have been done or words spoken before.

If this **philosophy** is correct, then it may be reasonable to believe that occasionally a supernatural **portal** opens through which **apparitions** can travel. Such a connection between the spirit world and ours is suggested by the term, *epiphany, a flash of insight or an experience that brings it [that insight] about.*

I had been working on this book for sometime when one day my wife asked a generic question about "the story." I don't really remember her specific question, nor do I remember my exact response. What I do remember, as I started to reply, was that a static shock flashed through my mind as if a switch had been closed and an electric circuit completed. For a split second, I was somewhere else, seeing images like a waking vision. Where? I am not sure. I either visited a familiar location or remembered a dream so vivid that at the time I thought it was real. As the image evaporated, I felt, rather than thought, *we have already had this conversation!* If I could have held onto that vision for a split second longer, I know I could have recalled all the details.

The reflection left as fast as it came. All that remained was an *I've already done this before* feeling. Frustrated with not being able to hold onto the perception, I turned to my wife and said "we've spoken these exact words before." We drove on in silence as we pondered the power of the **psyche**.

In the **spectrum** of life, could there be multiple energy levels, more than the length, width and depth dimensions that we can easily see and feel? A great deal of research has been done in the areas of **Extra Sensory Perception** or ESP. A concept that describes an area beyond our three **dimensional** world. If there are other degrees of existence, and we could examine them, what type of **persona** or force would be found?

So, my friend, as you read *An Allagash Haunting*, **contemplate**, just for a moment, the wonders of our universe and reflect on those places that hold special meaning, wherever that level of life's energy may be found.

Tim Caverly
Millinocket, Maine
September 2009

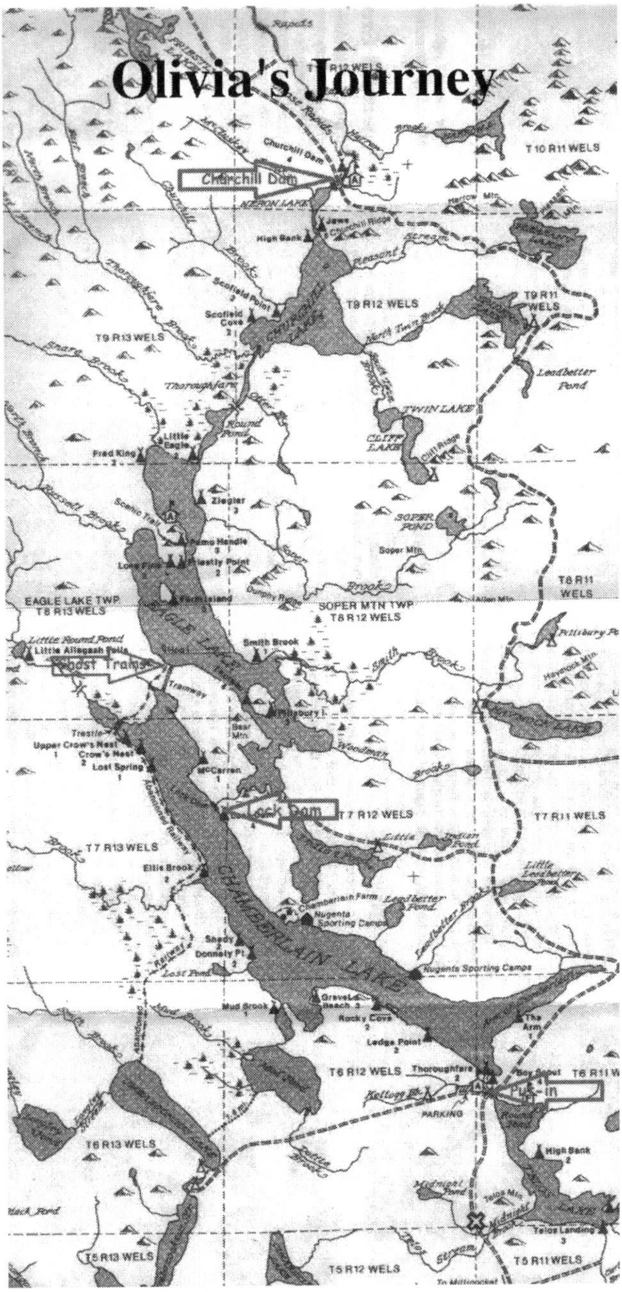
Olivia's Journey
Churchill Dam
T10 R11 WELS
High Bank
T9 R12 WELS
T9 R11 WELS
T9 R13 WELS
Scofield Cove
Leadbetter Pond
TWIN LAKE
CLIFF LAKE
Fred King
Little Eagle
Ziegler
SOPER POND
Soper Mtn
T8 R11 WELS
EAGLE LAKE TWP
T8 R13 WELS
SOPER MTN TWP
T8 R12 WELS
Smith Brook
Little Allagash Falls
Tramway
Pillsbury I.
Upper Crow's Nest
Crow's Nest
Lost Spring
Lock Dam
T7 R12 WELS
T7 R11 WELS
T7 R13 WELS
Ellis Brook
CHAMBERLAIN LAKE
Chamberlain Farm
Nugents Sporting Camps
Leadbetter Pond
Donnelly Pt
Mud Brook
Rocky Cove
Ledge Point
T6 R12 WELS
Thoroughfare
PARKING
Put-in
High Bank
T6 R13 WELS
Telos Landing
T5 R13 WELS
T5 R12 WELS
T5 R11 WELS

Eternal

Carried by the Winds of Time
Are Souls from Another Dimension.
Are They Friend or Are They Foe?
I Feel a Dark Apprehension!

—Tim Caverly
September 2009

I
A Storm Builds

"We'll just deal with whatever's comin!"
—Olivia's dad, Kevin, at Churchill Dam

Chapter I
A Storm Builds

It was late Saturday afternoon, and a storm was **brewing**. It wasn't the wimpy kind of soft rain that just limps in either, but a hard blow as if it had been cooked up in a **fermenting caldron**. Backed by gale-force winds, the black clouds were rolling. They were shoving aside, boiling over, and plowing each other under as they raced to obscure the day's light. It was a deep-breathing kind of storm that turns the sky into a trouble-brewing, pitch-black type of night that always seems to arrive on Halloween. It was a dampening cloak of darkness that was a breeding ground for apparitions. And ten-year-old Olivia was tent camping!

She didn't know what was coming but she certainly didn't like the looks of it. She felt **vulnerable** and she felt alone.

But Olivia wasn't alone. She was with her mother, father and their golden retriever on a **canoe** trip deep into the reaches of Maine's north woods. They were so far from the everyday sights and sounds of civilization that Olivia would stop and stare skyward anytime she heard, what had been before, the routine **drone** of an airplane.

Olivia had camped often, and usually she felt at home in "the back country." Her love for the outdoors came quite naturally; as a country music song might announce, it was a "family tradition."

Her thread with the forest began with her great grandparents. The great grandfather on one side had been a ranger with the Maine Forest Service. The other set of great grandparents had spent their whole lives in the woods working in the shadow of Mt. Katahdin in Baxter State Park, near Millinocket. Her great uncle had been Director of Baxter Park. Olivia's grandfather and grandmother had supervised the **Allagash Wilderness Waterway**, a nationally designated Wild and Scenic River, in the remote northwest corner of the state. Her mother, Jacquelyn, had moved into the Allagash country when she was only a week old and lived there for the first sixteen years of her life. But this trip to the woods was different. And here Olivia struggled to find the right description. She guessed that the word **mysterious** would just have to do.

A **loon** warned of the impending storm. A heavy south wind carried the **primeval** bird's call into the campsite with such force that her haunting cry **reverberated** throughout the forest. Smoke from the campfire reluctantly rose from the security of the fireplace and a full moon hid behind the clouds as if it were afraid of what it might see. A thick pea soup mist blanketed the ground.

This was the third night of Olivia's first canoeing trip down the Allagash, but tonight was the first time she felt troubled. Ever since she could remember, Olivia had heard **anecdotes** about this Wilderness Waterway. Her grandfather and grandmother had shared the wonderful adventures they had while living on the river and often told about all the good friends they had made. She had learned that her mother and father had canoed and camped on the Allagash more times than they could count. Even their dog, Allie, was named for Allagash Lake.

But she had never been this far into Maine's north woods before. Olivia knew that she was safe because she was with her parents and their dog. Nervously, she reminded herself that her mother, Jacquelyn, had grown up on the Allagash and knew the area by heart. She thought about her dad, Kevin, an accomplished outdoors person who spent every available minute hunting, fishing, or canoeing. They would make sure she was protected. Yet, something, yes *something* was different, very, very different….

II
Where Lumberjacks Slept

"Trust me, there is more to the Allagash than you can possibly imagine."
—Olivia's mom, Jacquelyn, at Chamberlain Bridge

Chapter II
Where Lumberjacks Slept

Their adventure had started Thursday, June twenty-fifth, when the family had launched their canoe at Chamberlain Bridge. The "put in" was located at the south end of eighteen-mile long Chamberlain Lake, at the beginning of the ninety-two-mile wilderness canoe trip. The first day, the wind had been at their backs, so they were able to reach the Lock Dam campsite, halfway down the lake, before dark. The second night, after a whole day of paddling north on bluebird-calm water and passing by Thoreau's Pillsbury

Island, the ghost trains and Farm Island, they arrived at the Pump Handle Campsite on Eagle Lake.

Olivia's mom was excited. Tomorrow would be Saturday, and they would be camping at Churchill **Dam**. Churchill was the beginning of the river portion of the trip. Long ago it had been the location of a very busy lumbering **depot**. It was where Jacquelyn had lived from 1982 to 1999. She wanted to point out her old **haunts**. Jacquelyn desired to take her family to such places as Morgan Island, and to show off nature's home. She wanted to watch the wildlife, the moose, deer, and geese that were always feeding at the mouth of McCluskey Brook. Most of all, she yearned to once again fall asleep to the night melodies of the loons. She wanted to revisit the log cabin that she called home until her late teens. Jacquelyn craved to walk the trails with her daughter that she had hiked as a child, the roadway to the dam, the old Jaws Lane to Churchill Lake, and the fern-crowded **portage** path to a bend in the river, known as the Big Eddy, just below Chase Rapids. Jacquelyn also was thrilled to reveal the boarding house.

When she was a little girl, Jacquelyn had delighted in the deserted **monstrosity** of the structure. Every time she entered the building, she felt a magical experience, as if she were stepping back in time. She inhaled old aromas and loved to **interpret** where the lumbermen had gathered around a huge wood stove to dry their wet clothing.

With the ancient smell of wet wool and unwashed feet, she'd imagined drying racks for red, green, and white double-knitted socks, soggy leather boots, and steaming **mackinaw** jackets. Strings of them must have been hung to recover from a frozen winter's day of cutting trees. She had seen the baked-on stains of tobacco juice splattered and dried on the sides of the woodstove as lumberjacks spit at this target while they spun their yarns. Jacquelyn could almost smell the baking of beans, biscuits, cookies, and pies as she walked through the old cook room. There on a dining room partition was nailed, in a place of honor, a torn and faded calendar. From the imprint on the wall, it was clear that the pages had gotten smaller over time as mice borrowed bits for their nests.

The first page of the calendar was stuck in time to the year 1925. The day, written in French, **Samedi le Juin** 27 was circled in red. From the kitchen Jacquelyn always went upstairs to the ram pasture.

The upstairs of this **dominant** old building was divided into two sections. The first, the ram pasture, was the larger room. This chamber **consumed** two-thirds of the second story. It was where the woodcutters slept. It was called the ram pasture because, like male sheep **thronged** in a pen, sometimes there had been so many men crowded together at night that it was impossible to slide even a piece of paper between the bed frames.

Walking up the stairs to the “pasture”, the old wooden steps creaked as if they needed to be oiled. Decades of lumberjacks, dragging weary foot after weary foot up the narrow corridor to fall exhausted into bed, had worn hollows into the center of the steps. At the top of the stairs, the room opened into a vast space. This was a huge bedroom, where the smell of liniment and perspiration hung in the stale air, as it mixed with the scent of the bats that now call the building home. Scratched in the paint on the floor were tracings where the cots had stood.

Smeared on the walls, over each bunk, were oval shaped grease spots from the lumberjack's unwashed hair as their heads had rested against the **wainscoting**.

Walking back down the stairs and through the kitchen, Jacquelyn weaved her way through years of stored debris towards another set of stairs that led up to the other second-story lodging. This section was much smaller than the first and had been partitioned into four rooms for those who had special duties around the village.

The first room was for the cook, arguably the most important person in camp. No one messed with the cook. At least lumberjacks didn't sass him if they wanted food that was hot, tasty, and served on time. Adjacent to the cook's room was Helen Hamlin's apartment. In 1945 Mrs. Hamlin had published a book, *Nine Mile Bridge*, which **chronicled** her life of living and teaching at Churchill Dam. Jacquelyn had always found Mrs. Hamlin's book about life at Churchill Dam, well… fitting. Next to Mrs. Hamlin's room was the **cubicle** of Emile Camile. Olivia had heard her mother speak of Emile Camile often, but it was odd. Whenever Olivia tried to ask questions about him, Mom would stare at a coin encased in plastic on their fireplace mantel, smile strangely, and say, "Not now dear. I'll tell you someday, but not today." Then Jacquelyn would add in a fading voice, "When it is time," ending softly, "when it is time."

When she was three, Olivia had first heard about her mother living in the woods and the name of Emile Camile. She liked learning about nature and liked hearing the name of Emile Camile, because of the way the name rolled off her tongue, almost like poetry. As a little girl she had run around her parents living room, and in that three-year-old way, repeated, "Emile Camile, Emile Camile, Emile Camile," until she finally sat down exhausted, all the while laughing and giggling.

At the start of the trip, Mom had told Olivia that she had a treat for her family when they finally camped at the dam. She had told them she had a special activity planned but wouldn't say what it was. Olivia knew that her mother was full of surprises, and she couldn't wait to see what was in store.

III
The Third Day

"Why am I always so curious?"
— Olivia to her mom on Churchill Lake

Chapter III
The Third Day

Midmorning on Saturday, on the third day of the trip, the sky was starting to darken behind them as they paddled through Round Pond, northeast of Snare Brook. Suddenly twenty-seven Canadian Geese launched from the grassy shore, and with beating wings, flew mutely north, as if they had remembered a forgotten appointment and couldn't spare the time for conversation. Kevin wondered silently as he remembered that this was the twenty-seventh day of the month, *that's odd, why wasn't there twenty, twenty-five or even thirty geese, but why exactly 27, why today? Just* ***coincidence****, that's all, just purely coincidence*, he assured himself.

Late that afternoon they paddled across Heron Lake and headed toward the landing at the dam. Allie was constantly sniffing the air as if she were looking for something that was out there. As they drifted along, it was obvious they were coming to a place where something had happened.

When they floated by the supervisor's headquarters on the east shore of Heron Lake, Jacquelyn pointed to the old log home where she used to live. Near the path to the cabin, the family noticed six Red Wing Blackbirds oddly lined up on an alder branch, watching their passage with deafening silence. Once again Kevin quietly questioned, *first twenty-seven geese and now six blackbirds and this is the month of June, could there be an* ***omen*** *here?* He promptly **liberated** the idea as doubtful, drove his paddle deep into the water, and propelled their canoe towards the dock.

The dam by itself was an imposing structure that seemed to rise straight out of the water. But there was a lot more. A canoe launch area, a ranger station, a hulking old supply shed left over from the lumbering days, and a campsite. Directly behind the campsite was…the Boarding House.

They carried their gear to the picnic table on the campsite, watching fearfully over their shoulders, as the storm hastened from the south to catch up. Kevin and

Jacquelyn wanted to set up camp and tie down the tarps before the heavy wind and rain that was sure to come. They could hear bits of the old building's asphalt siding flapping as the wind built with force. Kevin, with a **furrowed** brow, worried out loud, to no one in particular, "Yes-sir-ree, it looks to be building into a powerful storm. As Kevin Mannix, the Channel Six TV weather man, might announce in that, *you pay attention now*, voice, A severe storm warning *is* in effect, folks." Kevin smiled to himself, proud of his only slightly imperfect impersonation. After they finished setting up camp, they donned their raincoats and went exploring before dark took over.

Despite being in the heart of the Maine

woods, the boarding house was an impressive structure. It was a long barracks of a building; two stories high and measured one hundred feet long by twenty-four feet wide. There were rows of windows on all sides, and three sets of double doors along the front. The **ramshackle** sides of the building were sheathed with green asphalt shingles and capped off with a buckled tin roof. The building shouldered an old log-hauling road.

As the family walked up toward the rickety porch, they noticed the building was showing its age. The work camp seemed bent, as someone who suffers from a bad back. The roofline had sagged in a bow over the windows. The stress to the building forced the windows into an oval shape. The years of a rotting foundation made the double doors lopsided, which gave the whole building the appearance of, well, frowning. Hesitantly, Jacquelyn led her family inside, but the door was barricaded with a huge brass padlock.

A posted sign ominously announced

NO TRESPASSING
BY ORDER OF
THE STATE OF MAINE

She wasn't sure if she should be disappointed or relieved that her family couldn't go in.

The rains never came. After a late supper, the thunderheads cleared and the wind collapsed like one who crumples into their favorite chair after a long day at work. As dark fell, the full moon gained confidence to light their encampment. The campfire, as if realizing that everything was going to be okay, relaxed to glowing embers.

Jacquelyn disappeared into the tent, and in a short time returned carrying a package. In the bundle were a number of stories about the Allagash. Some were children's stories that her father had written about beavers, bears, and ducks. But the publication Mom pulled out tonight was a newspaper article, yellowed with age, pages worn thin from reading and stained from late night reflections over coffee.

Years before, a famous Maine author had broken the story about the ghost of Emile Camile. It was that story that Jacquelyn had brought back to the Allagash to share with her family. Jacquelyn unfolded the newspaper and read....

An Allagash Haunting

IV
The Article

"I think I've discovered the secret to the road of life.
Just don't get stuck in the potholes"
—Olivia's grandmother, Susan

Chapter IV
The Article

REAL GHOST HAUNTS CHURCHILL DAM!

by Gil Gilpatrick—Maine Sportsman December 1991

There's a ghost stalking the shores of the Allagash Wilderness Waterway! No, he hasn't talked to me personally, but there can be no doubt – I have it firsthand from **infallible** sources. Let me tell you about it, but first a little background.

In the early 1930's Churchill Dam, or

Churchill Depot as it was known then, was a thriving little logging community. It was the hub of all the lumbering activities in the area, and as such was also the social center of the north woods. The families that lived there, mostly French-Canadian, inhabited one-and-a-half story houses, that were originally painted white, as well as in several log cabins. Scattered among these buildings were the usual assortment of hen houses, woodsheds, outhouses, garden plots and pigsties. On the same side of the river was a huge barracks-like building that housed the single men. It was called the bar-room and also served as a dining hall and, on occasion, a dance hall. It is one of the two buildings still standing today.

On the other side of the river was the business end of the operation. There were located the company office, a garage where Lombard tractors and other equipment were repaired, and a a storehouse containing huge quantities of molasses, salt pork, cases of canned goods, flour, sugar, salt, dried fruits, cereals, axes, rope, peaveys, tobacco, kerosene and everything else necessary to keep a community and a business in good running condition.

A day's work in those days was from daybreak to dark, and that didn't mean getting up at daybreak, it meant starting work at daybreak. As you might expect, with a work schedule like that, there would be men whose duties required them to be on the job even earlier and later, than the majority of the workers. One such man was the dam tender. His job was to get the river full of water before the drivers started sending logs down through the rock-strewn Chase Carry (Chase Rapids).

Emile Camile was all of four foot two inches tall, and like most of the folks at Churchill, he was French. Emile had been one heck of a riverman until two huge logs came together on his ankle and left him with a bad, and permanent, limp. Since then he tended the dam at Churchill and did odd jobs for the company when the dam didn't need his attention. Emile's **infirmity** had not **daunted** his spirit, however, and certainly not his love of fiddling at the Saturday-night dances in the Churchill boarding-house dining area. There, once each week, the tables were moved aside, and the back-woods community gathered for an evening of floor stomping to the music of two harmonicas and Emile's fiddle.

They all pranced and pounded the *Boston Fancy, Lady of the Lake, Soldier's Joy, Sashay Up and Sashay Down, Four Hands Around*, and *Dive and Six*. The dances were called partly in English and partly in French, and through it all Emile fiddled and stamped his good foot in time to the music as the dancers spun and whirled across the cornmeal-powdered floor. It was his greatest moment – the thing he lived and worked for the rest of the week.

Early one Saturday morning in May, Emile limped his way to the dam to complete his usual ritual of opening the gates to provide water for the day's work of log driving. The night had been cold and a freezing rain had left the trees and everything else covered with a thick layer of ice. He slipped some along the ice-covered path to the dam, but he managed to stay upright by keeping to the relative safety of the grass along the side of the path. Even as he made his way to the dam, slipping and sliding in the pre-dawn darkness, he was thinking of the dance to come that night when the day's work was done. He had spent the evening before fondly checking over his fiddle, making sure everything was just right. Not that it needed any attention, but handling his precious instrument made the anticipation of the coming festivities all the more exciting.

The gate structure at the dam, like everything else that morning, was ice-covered. The first gate was partly open, but it would have to run wide open until the workday was done. As Emile approached the wheel that was used to raise the first gate, he took a moment to kick ice from the timber where he had to stand to turn the wheel.

This done, he stepped up on it, ready to start the long process of turning up the gate. As he turned to face the wheel, his good foot came down on a piece of ice. He slipped and did not have the strength in his bad leg to regain his balance. Instinctively he grabbed for the wheel, but it too was ice covered and offered no gripping surface. Emile fell into the **sluiceway** that was running cold and fast into the rapids below. No one would know of Emile's fate until the men went to work at daybreak only to find the gates had not been opened.

Well, that's how it happened, but guess what? *Emile Camile still fiddles at Churchill Dam!* This past summer, the Allagash work crews, in the course of their work, stayed where the job took them. If need be, they camped in tents, but if a waterway building was available, they lived in that.

Understandably, they preferred the relative comfort of solid walls and roof.

While working at Churchill, the group stayed in the old bar-room (bunkhouse). Late one Saturday night, *all of them* woke up to fiddle music coming from somewhere in the dark building. There were four or five of them, they all heard it, and all reacted the same. They got out of there, preferring the discomfort of tents and sleeping on the ground to sharing quarters with a fiddling ghost.

But that's not the end of it. With the cat out of the bag, so to speak, a receptionist at Churchill Dam for Allagash Wilderness Waterway admitted to seeing strange lights in the bar-room from her cabin directly across the river. Thinking back, she supposes it was always on a Saturday night.

So, there you have it. The spirit of the old logging days appears to be alive and well at Churchill Dam – you never know….

V
Pitou

"Ah, there is more magic in music than you can possibly know!"
— Mrs. Emile Camile

CHAPTER V
Pitou

For quite some time, neither Kevin, Jacquelyn, nor Olivia spoke; they just stared at the dying embers of the fire. Finally, Olivia broke the silence and asked all at once, “Mom have you seen the lights? Have you ever heard the music? Have you seen Emile Camile?”

Jacquelyn replied softly, “What do you think, dear? You don’t think there are any such things as ghosts, do you?” But Olivia noticed a strange twinkle in her mother’s eye as Jacquelyn looked at Olivia inquiringly, as if wondering, could this be the night? But it was time for bed.

Kevin shut off the **Coleman lantern** and by flashlight the three people crawled into the tent and snuggled deep into their sleeping bags. As the dog crawled in beside Olivia, they listened to the **peepers** singing their song for tomorrow.

Before long Olivia heard her parents whispering softly, the quiet kind of talk that parents often have when it is best the child doesn't hear. Then Olivia heard their conversation turn to sounds of deep slumber. Allie whimpered in her sleep as she dreamed of chasing imaginary squirrels. Soothed by the aroma of the spruce wind, Olivia watched the moon through the tent window. Snuggled in her sleeping bag, she patted Allie's head and contemplated the story of Emile Camile.

Just as Olivia was nodding off to sleep, she heard a noise outside the tent. It sounded like the shuffling of feet and the clanging of a metal teapot being knocked off a picnic table.

Afraid that raccoons had opened their cooler and were ransacking their food, she decided to make one last check of their equipment. Quietly, so as not to wake her parents, she climbed out of her sleeping bag, pulled on a sweatshirt to protect her from the night chill, and stepped outside. Allie sat up and watched Olivia closely, ready to follow on command. Olivia softly ordered, "Stay girl!" Allie immediately lay down, eyes **riveted** on the girl, the dog's muscles **taut**, ready to spring at the first sign of being needed.

The high beam from the moon lit the way for her inspection. Olivia didn't see any sign of animal vandals bothering their food, so she turned toward the tent to recapture the warmth of her sleeping bag. As she revolved, she caught the reflection of a light radiating from inside the boarding house and the brief sound of melody before it was hauled away by the wind. *Was there? No it couldn't be! The light must have been the reflection of the moon off the windows. The music was probably just the wind whistling through the cracks of the old tin roof,* she thought.

"Bon soir, ma chère," a voice behind her said gently. Startled, Olivia's hair rose on the back of her neck as she spun toward the sound. There at the corner of the fireplace stood a man. Not a tall man, but nevertheless someone who shouldn't be there.

"May I sit down, **Mademoiselle**?" He asked politely in a broken mixture of French and English, as he limped toward one of the seats at the picnic table.

Olivia nodded yes without speaking.

She wondered, *Should she wake her parents? Why wasn't Allie barking? The dog has always protected her before!*

"No you don't need to, they are tired. I will not hurt you, ma **petit**," the stranger responded as if reading her mind. "Allie is okay. She knows that I am a friend," the man continued.

Olivia realized that Allie was strangely quiet, not even issuing an inquiring woof.

Pale in appearance, he was a short, handsome man with soft brown eyes. His coal-black hair was freshly brushed, and he sported a handlebar mustache. He wore a checkered woolen shirt, green breeches, and smelled of **talcum** powder. Despite his weak foot, he moved to the picnic table with purpose, as if accustomed to moving around the thick woods.

"Well, **allô**, Olivia," the man offered in a soft voice.

"How do you know my name? she asked. "Have I met you before?"

"Non, we aren't acquainted," explained the man. "But I am a friend of **ta mére**, Jacquelyn, and I heard you were coming. Your mother and I met many years ago when she was just a little bit older than you are now. She was a **bonne amie**."

"How do you know my mother? Are you canoeing the Allagash, too? What is your name? Is your family with you? Where are you camped?" Olivia whispered excitedly. She knew there wasn't supposed to be anyone else camping on the site that night. Questions flooded her mind like a swollen stream after a heavy rain. *Who was this man? Why was he here? What did he want?*

"My nickname is **Pitou**, and I will answer all your questions in good time. I had twelve children of my own and a dear, dear wife. And no they are not with me, but I miss them terribly," said Pitou. "You see," he sadly continued, "I had a small accident several years ago and have been unable to see them again. But enough of that," he dismissed, "for tonight is a special night. Will you take **une** petit walk with me, **s'il vous plaît**?" Pitou's face brightened as he added, "I want to show you something. We are not going that far, just to the boarding house. You will enjoy the experience more than you can possibly believe."

As he explained, "Your mother used to come visit with me, and sometimes she would explain to guests about our life in the boarding house. Frequently she came back, after the others had left, and would talk with me. Sometimes the woods can be a lonely place for a little girl, but she was always very nice. We spoke often. I have missed her; I haven't had anyone from this time period who has talked to me in a long while."

For some reason Olivia felt very comfortable with Pitou. It was as if she had known him forever; instinctively she knew there was nothing to fear and agreed to walk with him.

VI
Saturday Night

"Hey, wait a minute dude!
If it starts with spooky, creepy or "forbidden"
in the adventure, I ain't goin."
—Allie the golden retriever at Churchill Dam

CHAPTER VI
Saturday Night

"**Très bien**," he muttered as he took her hand and limped up the **compacted** path beside her. As they walked toward the old structure, a **billowing** ground vapor parted as a portal bidding them to enter. When they got close, Olivia could see that there were lights on in the cook room and the dining area. She heard a faint harmony in the air. When they rounded the corner of the building, Olivia could see that improvements had been made.

But when? she wondered. She had not heard any equipment and had not seen anyone working. The road had been freshly graded; the building now stood tall and proud with a fresh coat of white paint. The doors and windows had been fixed and the building appeared to be…smiling.

As they climbed the steps, Olivia could smell the warm aroma of food baking. They peered through the freshly washed windows of the door into the dining area. The tables and benches had been pushed against the walls. The room was painted battleship gray and the floors, a shrieking orange. Yellow curtains gently drifted in the breeze of the open windows. There were dozens and dozens of people talking in small groups throughout the kitchen. The tables sagged **luxuriously** under the weight of jars of pickles, plates of **créton** and crackers, baked hams, pots of beans, **ploys**, jugs of maple syrup as well as cartwheel, molasses, and filled cookies.

On the floor, by the edge of the table, was an **ice cream churn** packed solid with rock salt and ice, dusted with sawdust. And there were pies. Just look at the pies; there were dried apple, blueberry, raspberry, raisin, and sugar pies. Centered on the wall behind the table hung a large fresh white calendar with the date, Samedi le 27 Juin 1925 circled in red.

At one end of the room there were two people impatiently tapping their harmonicas as a fiddle stood woefully alone, propped up in a chair. Others with guitars and **guimbardes** watched the door and paced nervously as if waiting for someone. The people in the room wore all manner of dress. The men wore everything from checkered shirts and breeches to suits. Some women wore green paisley print dresses; others wore pink skirts and sweaters. All the ladies were adorned with greasy cosmetics highlighted by necklaces, earrings, bracelets, and flashy pins.

When Pitou neared the door several of the men waved and one hollered at him, "**Entrez**, Emile, **vite se dépêcher**—hurry up! **Tout le monde veut dancer**." (Everyone wants to dance.)

"Where have you been? It is your time to fiddle and to do the **gigue**!"

The man turned and said to Olivia, "I will go in now, for I have to make the music. You are welcome to watch, but you *must not* follow. I am glad you are here. I hope you come back to see me. Give your mother a big hug for me, and here is a present for you," he said as he handed her a onecent coin. The money was stamped with Canada across the top, a maple leaf on each side and the year 1925 on the bottom.

"Th..th…thank you," she stammered, overwhelmed with the whole experience as she accepted the gift. As Pitou left, he patted her arm like a grandfather saying goodbye to a granddaughter. His hand felt cold but his expression was warm. A smile radiated from his mouth to his eyes and he gently offered "**Au revoir**, for now. Come back again for there is much to learn here." As Olivia watched him hobble inside, she absent-mindedly placed the coin in her sweatshirt pocket.

The time passed quickly as she watched the festivities through that little window. She became hypnotized by the sights and sounds. The French music surrounded her with songs she had never heard before, in words that she didn't understand. Yet the tunes were so lively and quick that her feet tapped in time to the music as she stared through the door's panes of glass. Every once in a while Pitou would throw down his fiddler's bow and jump into the middle of the floor and do the **jig**. Because his good foot was stronger than his bad foot, he would only dance in small circles. Now and then Pitou would glance up to see if Olivia was still there. He would smile each time he caught her eye.

Hours later, as the moon surrendered to daylight, Olivia heard a faded yelp from Allie, as if her bark were coming from a world beyond. The dog was looking for her. As she scurried back to the campsite, before Allie could wake her parents, a gentle enveloping mist bid her sad **adieux**.

With the smell of cookies and the sound of French songs still on her mind, she climbed back into her sleeping bag and fell asleep thinking about her new friend.

VII
The Rainbow

"The problem with dreams is that
you're never really sure if they were real or not!"
—Emile Camile

CHAPTER VII
The Rainbow

Later that morning, the sun's heat on the tent awoke Olivia to the crackling of a campfire and the smell of frying bacon. Her mother was making pancakes, and Olivia was eager to tell about her adventure. When she climbed out of the tent, she looked up at the boarding house.

Something had happened. Once again, the building sagged and the tattered green asphalt siding waved in the breeze. Without saying a word, and with Allie bounding beside her, she ran to the front of the structure.

The road was filled in with brush, as it had been the day before, and once again the building was padlocked. It seemed to be… sulking. Hadn't she heard music? She had seen a dance, hadn't she? Olivia couldn't have been dreaming! Could she?

Deep in thought, Olivia wandered at a snail's pace back to the campsite with Allie bumping her hand with her nose, asking to play. Olivia deliberately sat down at the picnic table and asked, "Mom, did **lumberjacks** ever wear talcum powder?"

Jacquelyn answered, "Yes, dear. The men use to wear it because they thought it would keep away the wood lice that used to frequent the old camps. But that was many years ago. No one uses it for that anymore, and they haven't for a very long time."

Olivia quietly ate breakfast, lost in thought, while her parents packed for the day's adventure. Today they were going to canoe **Class II** Chase **Rapids** and head for Umsaskis Lake. Jacquelyn watched Olivia closely and smiled secretively to herself as she put her hand in her pocket and rubbed her lucky coin. At last she and Olivia could have that talk.

Olivia thought, *It had to be a dream! But it was a nice dream.* Chilled from the morning breeze, she placed her hands in the pockets of her sweatshirt. From there she pulled out a one-cent Canadian coin. It was adorned with maple leaves and was dated 1925. *How did that get there? Did her mother or father place it there?* she wondered. Then she remembered and clutched the coin tightly in her fist.

As they began down the rapids Olivia took one last look at the boarding house. She gasped.

There was a ***spectrum*** *of rainbow colors in a northern light* ***aurora emanating*** *from the forest behind the building. And there was a person inside the building, standing by the kitchen window, waving goodbye, wasn't there? No, there couldn't* *be, could there?*

But she shyly returned the wave, just in case. Olivia realized that she would be safe. But she could not help but sense, no it was a stronger feeling than that, she was certain that there was more, much more for her to discover along this spectacular river.

Olivia already knew she would return to the Allagash, soon, very, very soon. Who knows what doorway to life's experiences she might find on her next trip?

Friends

Conveyed by the Call of the Loon,
Pals from other dimensions,
Timelessly bump along,
And visit each generation.

–Tim Caverly
September 2009

VIII
EPILOGUE

Did the boarding house at Churchill Dam really exist? Absolutely. As of this writing it still stands, somewhat crooked but still on its foundation. An excellent description of logging life at Churchill Dam may be found in Helen Hamlin's book, *Nine Mile Bridge.*

Was there really an Emile Camile? I am not certain. I thought that this character was purely fictional, being a **compilation** of woods characters I have met and read about during the thirty-five years I've enjoyed going to the Allagash Wilderness Waterway. But maybe, his spirit haunts even me; informing me.

Was there a real newspaper article written about the incident? Yes. It appeared in the *Maine Sportsman* in 1991, written by outdoor author, Master Maine Guide and good friend, Gil Gilpatrick.

Did the state workers see a ghost and hear music that night so long ago when they were staying in the boarding house? Well, they thought they did. That is why, in the dark of night, they moved out of the building and set up tents.

Did Olivia, Jacquelyn, and Kevin have

a similar experience? Not that I am aware of. I just thought it would be fun to tell the tale as if my granddaughter, daughter and son-in-law had lived it.

Although this story has a sprinkling of truth, it is an Allagash Tall Tale. However a few weeks after the article appeared in the paper, Gil received the following letter:

1-16-92

Bon Jour Monsieur Gil,

Your beautiful story about my cher Emile brought tears to my eyes and to the twenty-four eyes of our twelve children. In your article you describe the real Emile. It seems like only yesterday that we would hear our dearest Emile limping to the kitchen door. I know he only came home in the spring and left in the fall, but that made his twice yearly visits all the more welcome. The family was so sad when we lost Emile in the accident. We were so proud of him and the music he could put together.

Oh how he liked to fiddle and to do the jig. If anything could make him come back, it would be his cher music. Sometimes Emile would get so taken up in his music that he would throw down the fiddle and dance and dance and dance.

Emile never let his bad leg get in the way of his dancing. Because his bad leg did not dance as good as his well leg, his well leg would dance faster than his bad leg. This always made him dance in petit cercle.

I remember that one night at Churchill Depot (Ville de Chien, we called it then) Emile had been fiddling to "The Jam on Garry's Rock." Well, during one inspiring lick, Emile threw down his fiddle and danced so hard and so quick that he actually screwed his back leg (the one with the brace) into the wooden floor. The music had to be stopped and Emile backed off before the dance could go on. Merci, Monsieur Gil, for telling the story of our cher Emile so well and bringing back fond memories. My family hope that you and Mrs. Gil sont très bien.

Sincerely,

Mme. Emile Camile

Despite my best efforts to create a fictional character, uncertainty remains if there is the ghost of a Mr. Camile out there. Or if other such spirits might exist in the dozens and dozens of old lumber camps scattered throughout the Maine woods in such places as Churchill Dam, Clayton Lake, and Seven Islands.

Regardless, strike up a conversation with anyone that knows about the Allagash and you will find such intensity and passion for the wilderness it represents, that it is reasonable to think that some people care for it so much that it is their peace on earth.

Tim Caverly
Millinocket, Maine
September 2009

Speaking of Peace On Earth in the Allagash

"There is too much beauty here to use it all."

—Father Alphie Marquis

The River

The spirit still lingers in a forest place,
Where one can dream a dream of
wilderness.

–Author Unknown
Date Unknown
Echo's Magazine

This story has received the

Misty the Golden Retriever
Playful bound of Approval.
AWARD

BIBLIOGRAPHY

Gilpatrick, Gil, Real Ghost Haunts
Churchill Dam, Maine Sportsman, December 1991

Hamlin, Helen, Nine Mile Bridge, W.W. Norton & Company. Inc, New York, New York, 1945.

Marquis, Alphie, Catholic Priest, In conversation with Supervisor Tim Caverly at High Bank Campsite on Churchill Lake, Allagash Wilderness Waterway. August, 1985

Author (unknown). The River. Echo Press, Inc. Date (unknown)

Emile Camile's Annotated GLOSSARY

A-B-C

adieux- {French} a farewell (plural form); saying goodbye to more than one person

Allagash Wilderness Waterway- a ninety-two mile wilderness canoe route in Northern Maine. A designated a wild river in the National Wild and Scenic River System.

allô- {French} hello

amie- {French}friend

anecdote- a short entertaining account of some event.

apparition- 1 anything that appears unexpectedly or strangely; 2 ghost; phantom

apprehension-1 perception or understanding; 2 fear; anxiety

au revoir- {French} goodbye

aurora- a luminous band in the night sky

billowing- a large wave; any large swelling mass or surge

bon / bonne- {French} good, valid

brew- 1. to be forming or gathering; be in preparation; 2. to boil, steep, soak or cook

caldron-1. a large kettle of water; 2. a state of violent agitation

canoe- a narrow, light boat moved by paddles

cercle- {French} circle

chère- {French} dear
chronicle- a historical record of events in the order in which they happened; record
Class II rapids- 1. moderate, medium-quick water in a river; 2. rapids with regular waves; clear and open passages between rocks and ledges; 3. maneuvering required
coincidence- the chance occurrence of two things at the same time or place in such a way as to seem remarkable.
Coleman lantern- a bright lamp usually used in camping, fueled by propane or Coleman fuel
compact- 1. closely and firmly packed; 2. taking little space
compile- to collect and sample data
consume- to use up or waste
contemplate-1. to look at or think about intently; 2. to expect or intend
créton- {French}pork spread with onions and spices
cubicle- a small compartment

D-E-F

dam- a barrier built to hold back flowing water
dancer- {French} dance
daunt- to intimidate or dishearten
déjà vu- a feeling of having been somewhere or experienced something before
depot-1. warehouse; 2. a storage place dimension- the amount of space occupied by something; an

area within which something or someone exists, acts, or has influence or power

dominant- 1. to rule or control by superior power; 2. to rise above the surroundings drone- to make a continuous humming sound

emanate- to come forth; issue, as from a source

entrer- {French} to enter; entrez=enter (imperative)

Extra Sensory Perception- ESP; commonly called the "sixth sense." Sensory information that an individual receives which comes beyond the ordinary five senses sight, hearing, smell, taste, and touch. It can provide the individual with information of the present, past, and future; as it seems to originate in a second, or alternate reality

ferment-1. excitement or agitation; 2. to be excited or agitated; seethe

furrow- as a deep wrinkle

G-H-I

generation- 1. all the people born and living at about the same time

gigue- {French} the jig

guimbarde- {French} Jew's harp. Also known as a jaw harp, or a mouth harp. Musical instrument, which consists of a flexible metal or bamboo tongue or reed attached to a frame. The sound is generated by a vibrating air column or by a stream of air stimulated to sound by a reed

(such as harmonica, accordion, jew's harp). The tongue/reed is placed in the performer's mouth and plucked with the finger to produce a note
haunt- to visit often; a place often visited

hypnosis- trancelike condition

ice cream churn- a machine that is hand cranked to stir a liquid ice cream mixture packed with salt and ice; used to produce homemade ice cream

infallible-1. incapable of error; 2. dependable

infirmity- physical weakness or defect

interpret- to explain or translate

J-K-L

jig- a fast springy dance in triple time

juin- {French} June

liberate- to release from occupation

loon- an aquatic fish-eating diving bird, considered to be of ancient heritage, it has a call described as an eerie yodel

lumberjack- person whose work is cutting down trees and sending logs to mills; logger

luxuriously- 1. fond of or indulging in luxury; 2. constituting luxury; rich; comfortable

M-N-O

ma- {French} my

mackinaw-{named after Mackinac Island in N Lake Huron} a short heavy, double-breasted woolen coat, usually plaid

mademoiselle- miss

Mme- {French} Mrs. [on letter]
monstrosity- 1. huge; enormous; 2. horrible; hideous; shocking
mysterious- 1. something unexpected or secret; 2. of, containing, implying, or characterized by mystery
non- {French} no
omen- a thing or happening supposed to foretell a future event, either good or evil

P-Q-R

paranormal- a general term that describes unusual experiences that lack a scientific explanation, or phenomena alleged to be outside of science's current ability to explain or measure
peepers- a small frog that makes short, high pitched sounds; ie spring peepers
persona- the mask or appearance one presents to the world
petit(e)- {French} small, little
phenomenon- 1. anything very unusual; 2. any observable fact or event that can be scientifically described
philosophy- the study of the principles underlying conduct, thought and the nature of the universe
Pitou- (French} nickname meaning "little man"
ployes- pancake-type mix of buckwheat flour and water. Popular in the St. John Valley of New Brunswick and Northern Maine
portage- the route by which canoes and supplies

are carried between navigable lakes and rivers.
portal- doorway or entrance
primeval- of the earliest times or ages
progression- 1. a moving forward; 2. continuing by successive steps
psyche- 1. the soul 2. the mind regarded as an entity based ultimately upon physical process but with its own complex processes
ramshackle- loose and rickety; likely to fall apart
reverberate- to re-echo or cause to re-echo
rapids- a river where the current is swift
riveted- fascinated with

S-T-U

samedi- {French} Saturday
sequence- the coming of one thing after another; the order in which this occurs
s'il vous plâit- {French} please / if it pleases you
sluiceway- 1. any artificial channel for water; 2.flow regulated by gate
soir- {French} evening
spectrum- 1 the series of colored bands separated and arranged in order of their respective wavelengths by the passage of white light through a prism; 2 a continuous range or entire extent
talcum powder- a powder for the body made of purified talc
taut- tightly stretched, tense
throng- 1 a crowd; 2 any great number of things

considered together

tout le monde- {French} everyone

très bien- {French}très=very; bien=well

une- {French} feminine a, an

V-W-X-Y-Z

vite se dépêcher- {French} hurry up

vulnerable- 1 that can be wounded or injured; 2 affected by a specified influence

wainscot- a wood paneling of a room, sometimes only on the lower part of a wall

About the Author: **Tim Caverly**

Photo by Ryan J. Moore Photography, Bucksport, Maine

Tim reading to baby Olivia, as a friend listens.

Tim has spent his life in Maine's outdoors. Growing up shadowing his father who was a fire warden with the Maine Forest Service and his brother, a ranger in Baxter State Park, it was natural for him to seek a career in the outdoors. Tim is from Skowhegan, Maine and has a Bachelor of Science Degree from the University of Maine at Machias.

While in college, Tim began working as a ranger at Sebago Lake State Park for the State Parks and Recreation Commission. After Sebago, he continued his employment with the Department of Conservation as manager of Aroostook and Cobscook Bay State Parks.

In 1999, Tim retired from the Department after a 32-year career and resides in Millinocket. He works in the Millinocket School System, and enjoys raising Golden Retrievers, and sharing stories about the Allagash.

About the Illustrator: **Franklin Manzo, Jr.**

Frank was born and raised in Millinocket, Maine where he attended several art classes at Stearns High School. Frank retired from his job as a software engineer after 25 years, and has worked as the Editor of a local weekly newspaper, is noted as a local photographer, and also works in the Millinocket School System. Frank has always enjoyed pursuing his art as a way of relaxing and was pleased to contribute the sketches used in this publication.

ALLAGASH
TAILS

Ask for all books in the Allagash Tails Collection
at your local bookstore.

Volume 1: **Allagash Tails – Marvin & Charlie** (Illustrated Children's Book)

A collection of tall tails for the whole family. Perfect to be read around the campfire or when tucking the little campers into bed. Swim with Marvin Merganser, a fish-eating bird that usually has very bad luck, but his sympathy for a watery neighbor changes all of that. Feel compassion for Charlie, the White Water Beaver. Charlie is cross-eyed and narrow tailed and dreams of a better life. See if he can overcome life's adversities in this charming "tail" for the ages.

Volume 3: **Wilderness Wildlife** — (Illustrated Children's Book)

Who was Henry David Thoreau anyway?

Ever since Henry David Thoreau visited the Allagash, thousands of people have flocked to Maine's North Woods to enjoy, deer, moose and the call of the loon. But do we really know what goes on in the animal world? What if we could talk to the animals, what might they say? Find out by reading "Wilderness Wildlife."

Float with Carl the Wise Old Canoe as he travels the Allagash and learns of the animal antics that his Allagash friends are having. Delight with Oscar "the awkward Osprey" when he falls out of the sky and finds the most unusual thing ever, astound to the chilling "tale" about how two young hunters tumble into trouble during The Attack at Partridge Junction. In the next edition of Allagash Tails enjoy the playful behavior of Oscar the Osprey as the learns to bellywaump. Float with Carl, the guides twenty-foot model canoe, as he discovers the new and unbelievable antics of his Allagash neighbors.

Volume 4: **A Wilderness Ranger's Journal – Rendezvous at Devil's Elbow** (Book Three of Olivia's Journey)
In the dark of night there is always something else!

There is a always special feeling to the Allagash (those of you who've been there know!); a sense of adventure, the thrill of getting away from it all!

In the sequel to the popular *An Allagash Haunting*, the family has only been on the water for four days and already Livy has experienced enough to last a lifetime.

In this mystery-adventure paddle with Olivia and her family as they canoe Northern Maine's most famous wilderness river, The Allagash. The three family members have only been on the river for four days and already they have experienced enough to last a life time. Looking at a map of their travel route they find there is a bend in the river called "The Devil's Elbow" in front of them. They wonder what they could possibly encounter next as the current carries them down stream against their will. In the darkest of the night, a shadow lingers, hiding beyond the reach of the lantern's fingers of light. It remains obscure in the midst of the evergreens and old growth. Among the campfires and s'mores, a bone-chilling draft embraces all. Shivering, we draw our coats tighter to protect against the rawness.

Volume 5: **Headin' North: A Tale of Two Diaries** (Book Three of Olivia's Journey)

Red sky at night,

Sailors delight
Red sky at morning,
Sailors take warning…
Remembering her grandfather's dire weather forecast, a young girl stares at the morning's inflamed sky. Traveling by canoe deep in the Maine woods is not where Olivia should be-but that's exactly where she is.

Suddenly— lightning strikes the nearby shore, nearly jumping the girl out of her skin. Looking towards the sound, the youth sees the apparition of a log cabin floating over a vacant lot. Inside the building a young ranger is looking out—the pair exchange unintended smiles—under the aroma of a blown out match, the scene fades.

This is the third and final book of the exciting North Maine Woods trilogy, detailing a family's paddle down a famous American River. During the day the girl records her unbelievably wild adventures, and each night she listens spellbound while her mother reads incredible tales from the grandfather's hand written journal. Olivia and her family are the 39 mile mark of a 92 mile wilderness Allagash canoe adventure. Then, in the middle of a remote lake they see storm clouds gathering. Thunderheads build and lightening strikes the nearby shore. Bolts of electricity char the ground, and the electric charge opens a portal through time. This cosmic doorway allows a granddaughter and grandfather, separated by the years, to write in their diaries at the same cosmic instant. In "*Headin' North*" discover stories from today and yesterday as Olivia experiences the North Maine Woods in a whole new way....and find out why Olivia feels like she is walking in her Pépé's (grandfather's) shoes…

Volume 6: **Solace**

During his third year of college a young man is forced to abandon school and leave his classmate and friend Susan behind. Jim returns to the family farm only to face one hardship after another. Broke and with debt mounting; Jim's world falls apart. Then one day, while cleaning out the attic of his now empty colonial home,

Jim discovers an envelope–yellowed with age.
The letter is from a grandfather he's never met and it instructs Jim to go to Allagash Lake and retrieve an heirloom "for the sake of the family!" Follow along as Jim treks deep into the Maine wilderness to recover a grandfather's keepsake and stumbles onto A mystical path to the past.
This is the sixth book in the *Allagash Tails Collection.* The story—While cleaning out an old family trunk, a grandson discovers unopened correspondence from his deceased grandfather. The letter instructs the young man to go to Allagash Lake to retrieve an heirloom "for the sake of the family." In this mystery adventure, canoe with Jim Clark as he searches for the bequest, and encounters a mystical energy highway where he learns more than he really cares to about the future.

Volume 7: **The Ranger and the Reporter**

Cub reporter Margaret Woodward has been given an assignment she doesn't want! The editor for the Penobscot Basin Times has sent her to interview retired ranger James Clark; a secretive Maine woodsman. Others' have tried to write the man's story; but none have been able to break through the outdoorsman's blunt exterior. Instructed to *complete the report* –Margaret visits Bangor's assisted living community; where "old man Clark is expected to live out his final days."
In this sequel to the popular book "*Solace*"–tag along with our reluctant newspaper trainee who struggles to uncover the mysterious ordeals of a wilderness ranger. Will she 'get her story' or will Margaret discover there is more to a person's life than waiting for an inscription on a tombstone—even hers?

Volume 8: **Andy's Surprise** (Illustrated Children's Book)

Andy -- What A Moose! Sometimes surprises can go two ways!
The story is about a Maine moose who one day receives the biggest surprise ever. Geared for the three-year old and up, the tale takes place in the heart of New England's wild river-the Allagash. The account is based on an event I witnessed one day when working as a Maine park ranger. The publication, an illustrated 600-word book, contains 16 full color drawings and 4 coloring

pages. 'Andy's Surprise' is perfect for the young of age and young of heart. All readers, in Maine or out of Maine, will enjoy this treasure from the wildest part of the northern woods.

ANNOUNCING

VOLUME NINE of The Allagash Tails Collection
'Tis The Season — Mainely
Published in the Fall of 2018

Visit us at
www.allagashtails.com

Also visit us at
www.leicesterbaybooks.com

Made in the USA
Lexington, KY
07 December 2019

58130563R00083